This is a Bleed Through Page If You Are Using a Colouring Marker or Pen!
Find Other Great Titles By searching for Bold Illustrations *on Your Favorite Book Retailer*
Amazon.Ca | Barnes & Noble (BN.Com) | Books A Million (BAM.Com)

Bold Illustrations
COLORING BOOKS

PIG COLORING BOOK!
DISCOVER THIS COLLECTION OF COLORING PAGES

Bold Illustrations
COLORING BOOKS

No part of this book may be reproduced or used in any way or form or by any means whether electronic or mechanical, this means that you cannot record or photocopy any material ideas or tips that are provided in this book.

Copyright 2018

This is a Bleed Through Page If You Are Using a Colouring Marker or Pen!
Find Other Great Titles By searching for Bold Illustrations *on Your Favorite Book Retailer*
Amazon.Ca | Barnes & Noble (BN.Com) | Books A Million (BAM.Com)

This is a Bleed Through Page If You Are Using a Colouring Marker or Pen!
Find Other Great Titles By searching for Bold Illustrations *on Your Favorite Book Retailer*
Amazon.Ca | Barnes & Noble (BN.Com) | Books A Million (BAM.Com)

Bold Illustrations
COLORING BOOKS

This is a Bleed Through Page If You Are Using a Colouring Marker or Pen!
Find Other Great Titles By searching for Bold Illustrations *on Your Favorite Book Retailer*
Amazon.Ca | Barnes & Noble (BN.Com) | Books A Million (BAM.Com)

Bold Illustrations
COLORING BOOKS

This is a Bleed Through Page If You Are Using a Colouring Marker or Pen!
Find Other Great Titles By searching for Bold Illustrations on Your Favorite Book Retailer
Amazon.Ca | Barnes & Noble (BN.Com) | Books A Million (BAM.Com)

This is a Bleed Through Page If You Are Using a Colouring Marker or Pen!
Find Other Great Titles By searching for Bold Illustrations on Your Favorite Book Retailer
Amazon.Ca | Barnes & Noble (BN.Com) | Books A Million (BAM.Com)

Bold Illustrations
COLORING BOOKS

This is a Bleed Through Page If You Are Using a Colouring Marker or Pen!
Find Other Great Titles By searching for Bold Illustrations on Your Favorite Book Retailer
Amazon.Ca | Barnes & Noble (BN.Com) | Books A Million (BAM.Com)

Bold Illustrations
COLORING BOOKS

This is a Bleed Through Page If You Are Using a Colouring Marker or Pen!
Find Other Great Titles By searching for Bold Illustrations on Your Favorite Book Retailer
Amazon.Ca | Barnes & Noble (BN.Com) | Books A Million (BAM.Com)

Bold Illustrations
COLORING BOOKS

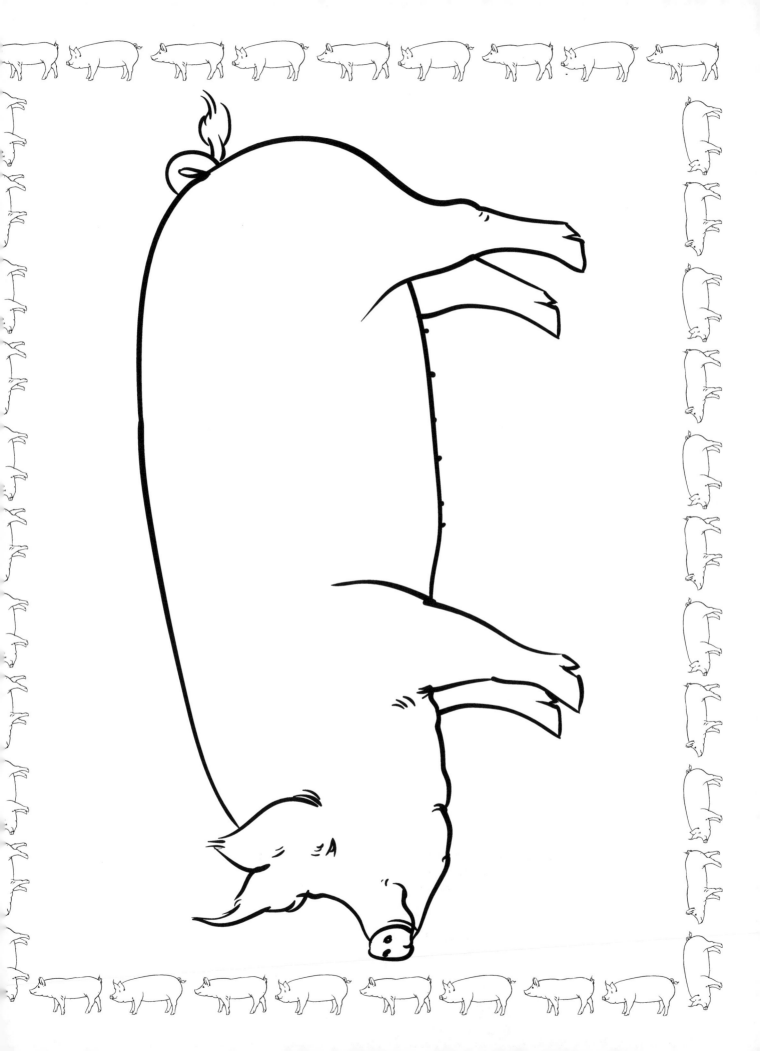

This is a Bleed Through Page If You Are Using a Colouring Marker or Pen!
Find Other Great Titles By searching for Bold Illustrations on Your Favorite Book Retailer
Amazon.Ca | Barnes & Noble (BN.Com) | Books A Million (BAM.Com)

Bold Illustrations
COLORING BOOKS

This is a Bleed Through Page If You Are Using a Colouring Marker or Pen!
Find Other Great Titles By searching for <u>Bold Illustrations</u> on Your Favorite Book Retailer
Amazon.Ca | Barnes & Noble (BN.Com) | Books A Million (BAM.Com)

Bold Illustrations
COLORING BOOKS

This is a Bleed Through Page If You Are Using a Colouring Marker or Pen!
Find Other Great Titles By searching for Bold Illustrations on Your Favorite Book Retailer
Amazon.Ca | Barnes & Noble (BN.Com) | Books A Million (BAM.Com)

This is a Bleed Through Page If You Are Using a Colouring Marker or Pen!
Find Other Great Titles By searching for Bold Illustrations on Your Favorite Book Retailer
Amazon.Ca | Barnes & Noble (BN.Com) | Books A Million (BAM.Com)

Bold Illustrations
COLORING BOOKS

This is a Bleed Through Page If You Are Using a Colouring Marker or Pen!
Find Other Great Titles By searching for Bold Illustrations on Your Favorite Book Retailer
Amazon.Ca | Barnes & Noble (BN.Com) | Books A Million (BAM.Com)

Bold Illustrations
COLORING BOOKS

This is a Bleed Through Page If You Are Using a Colouring Marker or Pen!
Find Other Great Titles By searching for Bold Illustrations on Your Favorite Book Retailer
Amazon.Ca | Barnes & Noble (BN.Com) | Books A Million (BAM.Com)

Bold Illustrations
COLORING BOOKS

This is a Bleed Through Page If You Are Using a Colouring Marker or Pen!
Find Other Great Titles By searching for Bold Illustrations on Your Favorite Book Retailer
Amazon.Ca | Barnes & Noble (BN.Com) | Books A Million (BAM.Com)

Bold Illustrations
COLORING BOOKS

This is a Bleed Through Page If You Are Using a Colouring Marker or Pen!
Find Other Great Titles By searching for Bold Illustrations on Your Favorite Book Retailer
Amazon.Ca | Barnes & Noble (BN.Com) | Books A Million (BAM.Com)

Bold Illustrations
COLORING BOOKS

This is a Bleed Through Page If You Are Using a Colouring Marker or Pen!
Find Other Great Titles By searching for Bold Illustrations *on Your Favorite Book Retailer*
Amazon.Ca | Barnes & Noble (BN.Com) | Books A Million (BAM.Com)

Bold Illustrations
COLORING BOOKS

This is a Bleed Through Page If You Are Using a Colouring Marker or Pen!
Find Other Great Titles By searching for Bold Illustrations on Your Favorite Book Retailer
Amazon.Ca | Barnes & Noble (BN.Com) | Books A Million (BAM.Com)

Bold Illustrations
COLORING BOOKS

This is a Bleed Through Page If You Are Using a Colouring Marker or Pen!
Find Other Great Titles By searching for <u>Bold Illustrations</u> on Your Favorite Book Retailer
Amazon.Ca | Barnes & Noble (BN.Com) | Books A Million (BAM.Com)

Bold Illustrations
COLORING BOOKS

This is a Bleed Through Page If You Are Using a Colouring Marker or Pen!
Find Other Great Titles By searching for <u>Bold Illustrations</u> on Your Favorite Book Retailer
Amazon.Ca | Barnes & Noble (BN.Com) | Books A Million (BAM.Com)

Bold Illustrations
COLORING BOOKS

This is a Bleed Through Page If You Are Using a Colouring Marker or Pen!
Find Other Great Titles By searching for Bold Illustrations on Your Favorite Book Retailer
Amazon.Ca | Barnes & Noble (BN.Com) | Books A Million (BAM.Com)

Bold Illustrations
COLORING BOOKS

This is a Bleed Through Page If You Are Using a Colouring Marker or Pen!
Find Other Great Titles By searching for Bold Illustrations on Your Favorite Book Retailer
Amazon.Ca | Barnes & Noble (BN.Com) | Books A Million (BAM.Com)

Bold Illustrations
COLORING BOOKS

This is a Bleed Through Page If You Are Using a Colouring Marker or Pen!
Find Other Great Titles By searching for Bold Illustrations on Your Favorite Book Retailer
Amazon.Ca | Barnes & Noble (BN.Com) | Books A Million (BAM.Com)

Bold Illustrations
COLORING BOOKS

This is a Bleed Through Page If You Are Using a Colouring Marker or Pen!
Find Other Great Titles By searching for Bold Illustrations on Your Favorite Book Retailer
Amazon.Ca | Barnes & Noble (BN.Com) | Books A Million (BAM.Com)

Bold Illustrations
COLORING BOOKS

This is a Bleed Through Page If You Are Using a Colouring Marker or Pen!
Find Other Great Titles By searching for Bold Illustrations on Your Favorite Book Retailer
Amazon.Ca | Barnes & Noble (BN.Com) | Books A Million (BAM.Com)

Bold Illustrations
COLORING BOOKS

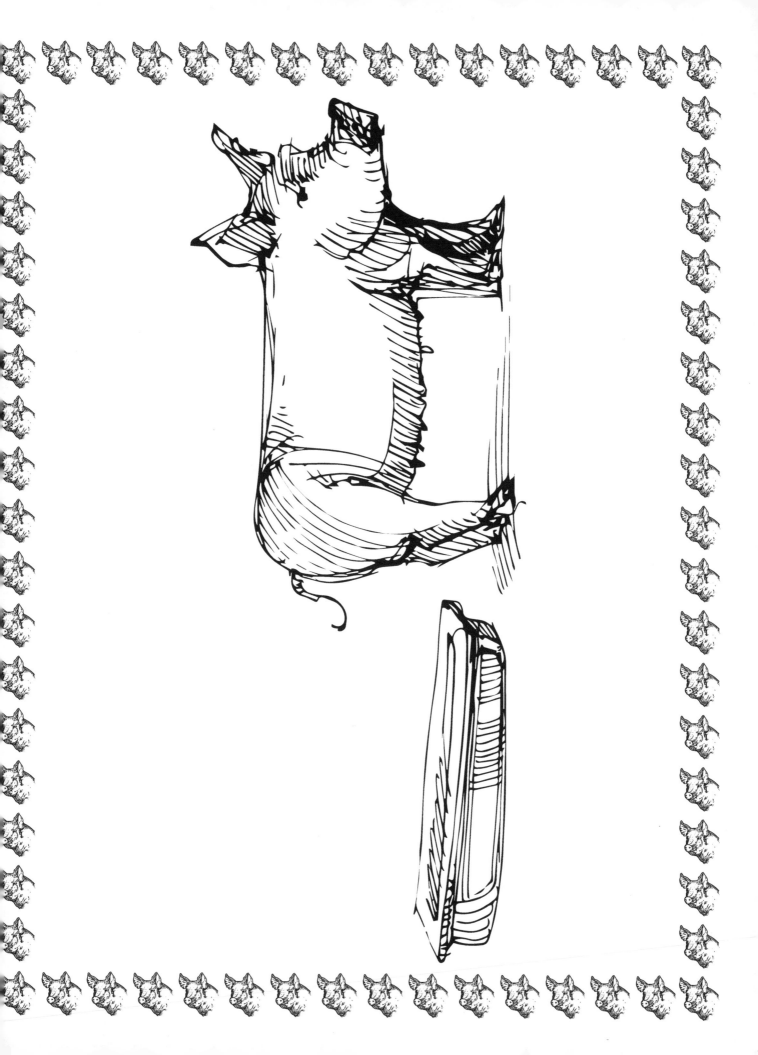

This is a Bleed Through Page If You Are Using a Colouring Marker or Pen!
Find Other Great Titles By searching for Bold Illustrations on Your Favorite Book Retailer
Amazon.Ca | Barnes & Noble (BN.Com) | Books A Million (BAM.Com)

This is a Bleed Through Page If You Are Using a Colouring Marker or Pen!
Find Other Great Titles By searching for Bold Illustrations on Your Favorite Book Retailer
Amazon.Ca | Barnes & Noble (BN.Com) | Books A Million (BAM.Com)

Bold Illustrations
COLORING BOOKS

This is a Bleed Through Page If You Are Using a Colouring Marker or Pen!
Find Other Great Titles By searching for Bold Illustrations *on Your Favorite Book Retailer*
Amazon.Ca | Barnes & Noble (BN.Com) | Books A Million (BAM.Com)

Bold Illustrations
COLORING BOOKS

This is a Bleed Through Page If You Are Using a Colouring Marker or Pen!
Find Other Great Titles By searching for Bold Illustrations on Your Favorite Book Retailer
Amazon.Ca | Barnes & Noble (BN.Com) | Books A Million (BAM.Com)

Bold Illustrations
COLORING BOOKS

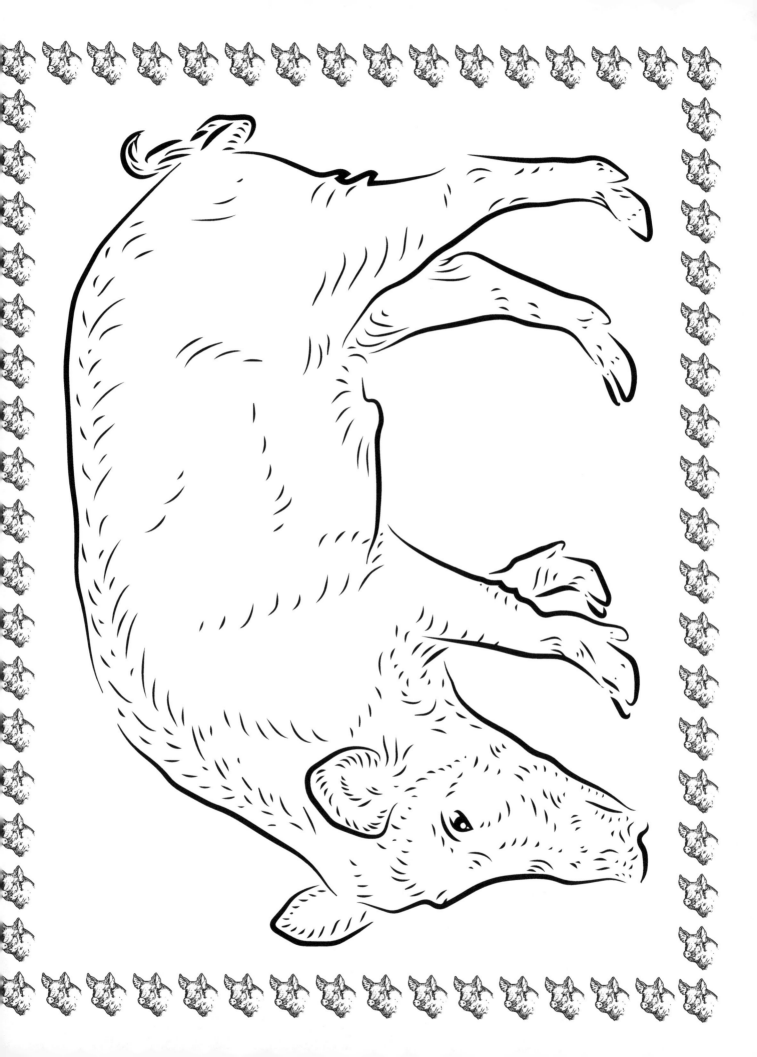

This is a Bleed Through Page If You Are Using a Colouring Marker or Pen!
Find Other Great Titles By searching for Bold Illustrations on Your Favorite Book Retailer
Amazon.Ca | Barnes & Noble (BN.Com) | Books A Million (BAM.Com)

Bold Illustrations
COLORING BOOKS

This is a Bleed Through Page If You Are Using a Colouring Marker or Pen!
Find Other Great Titles By searching for Bold Illustrations *on Your Favorite Book Retailer*
Amazon.Ca | Barnes & Noble (BN.Com) | Books A Million (BAM.Com)

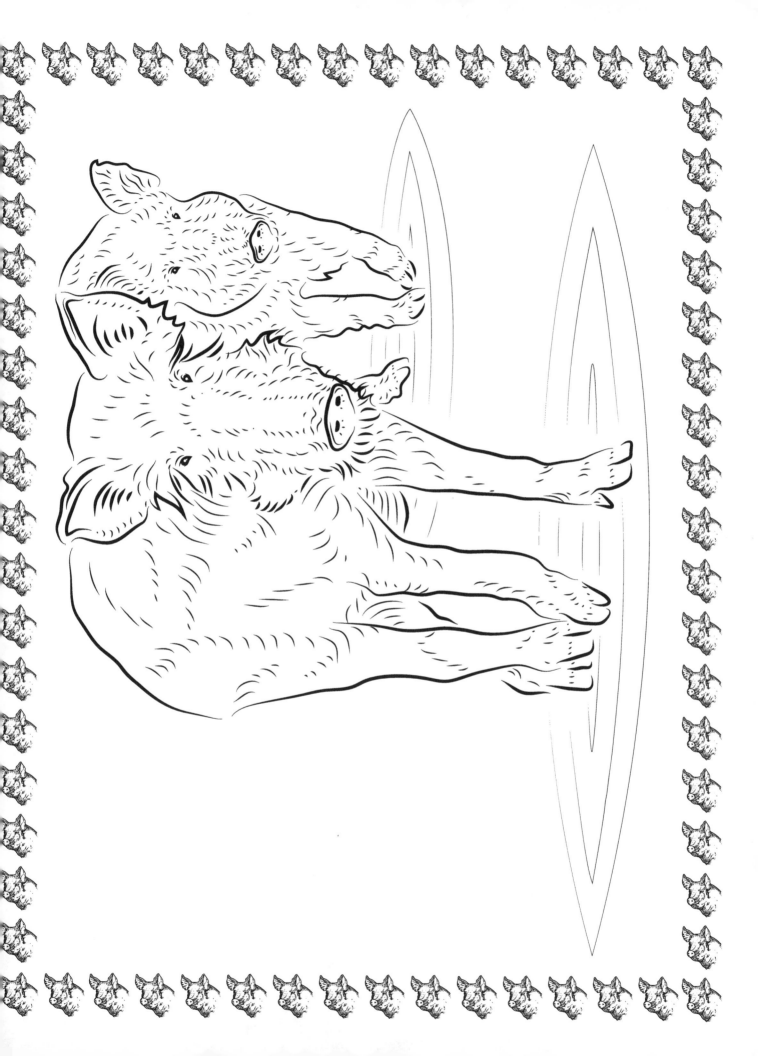

This is a Bleed Through Page If You Are Using a Colouring Marker or Pen!
Find Other Great Titles By searching for Bold Illustrations on Your Favorite Book Retailer
Amazon.Ca | Barnes & Noble (BN.Com) | Books A Million (BAM.Com)

Bold Illustrations
COLORING BOOKS

This is a Bleed Through Page If You Are Using a Colouring Marker or Pen!
Find Other Great Titles By searching for Bold Illustrations on Your Favorite Book Retailer
Amazon.Ca | Barnes & Noble (BN.Com) | Books A Million (BAM.Com)

Bold Illustrations
COLORING BOOKS

This is a Bleed Through Page If You Are Using a Colouring Marker or Pen!
Find Other Great Titles By searching for Bold Illustrations on Your Favorite Book Retailer
Amazon.Ca | Barnes & Noble (BN.Com) | Books A Million (BAM.Com)

Bold Illustrations
COLORING BOOKS

This is a Bleed Through Page If You Are Using a Colouring Marker or Pen!
Find Other Great Titles By searching for Bold Illustrations on Your Favorite Book Retailer
Amazon.Ca | Barnes & Noble (BN.Com) | Books A Million (BAM.Com)

Bold Illustrations
COLORING BOOKS

This is a Bleed Through Page If You Are Using a Colouring Marker or Pen!
Find Other Great Titles By searching for Bold Illustrations on Your Favorite Book Retailer
Amazon.Ca | Barnes & Noble (BN.Com) | Books A Million (BAM.Com)

This is a Bleed Through Page If You Are Using a Colouring Marker or Pen!
Find Other Great Titles By searching for Bold Illustrations on Your Favorite Book Retailer
Amazon.Ca | Barnes & Noble (BN.Com) | Books A Million (BAM.Com)

Made in the USA
Coppell, TX
21 November 2023

24569009R00042